JABARI JUMPS

To Larkin, who is already a great jumper,
and to her big brother, Rowan,
who uses his "bravery" every day

First published 2017 by Walker Books Ltd, 87 Vauxhall Walk, London SE11 5HJ • This edition published 2018 • © 2017 Gaia Cornwall • The right of Gaia Cornwall to be identified as author and illustrator of this work has been asserted by her in accordance with the Copyright, Designs and Patents Act 1988 • This book has been typeset in Lora • Printed in China • All rights reserved. No part of this book may be reproduced, transmitted or stored in an information retrieval system in any form or by any means, graphic, electronic or mechanical, including photocopying, taping and recording, without prior written permission from the publisher. • British Library Cataloguing in Publication Data: a catalogue record for this book is available from the British Library • ISBN 978-1-4063-8087-3 • www.walker.co.uk • 10 9 8 7 6 5 4 3 2

JABARI JUMPS

Gaia Cornwall

WALKER BOOKS
AND SUBSIDIARIES

LONDON · BOSTON · SYDNEY · AUCKLAND

"I'm jumping off the diving board today," Jabari told his dad.
"Really?" said his dad.

The diving board was high and maybe a little scary, but Jabari had finished his swimming lessons and passed his swim test, and now he was ready to jump.

"I'm a great jumper," said Jabari, "so I'm not scared at all."

Jabari watched the other kids climb the long ladder. They walked all the way out to the end of the board, as big as tiny bugs. Then they stood on the edge. They spread their arms and bent their knees. And sprang up! up! up! And then they dove down, down, down.

Splash!

"Looks easy," Jabari said.

But when his dad squeezed his hand, Jabari squeezed back.

Jabari stood at the bottom of the ladder.
He looked up.

"You can go before me if you want," he told the kid behind him.

"I need to think about what kind of special jump I'm going to do."

Jabari thought and thought.

Jabari started to climb. Up and up.
This ladder is very tall, he thought.

"Are you OK?" called his dad.

"I'm just a little tired," said Jabari.

"Maybe you should climb down and
take a tiny rest," said his dad.

A tiny rest sounded like a good idea.

When he got to the bottom, Jabari remembered something.
"I forgot to do my stretches!" he said to his dad.

"Stretching is very important," said his dad.

"I think tomorrow might be a better day
   for jumping," Jabari said.

They looked up at the diving board
together.

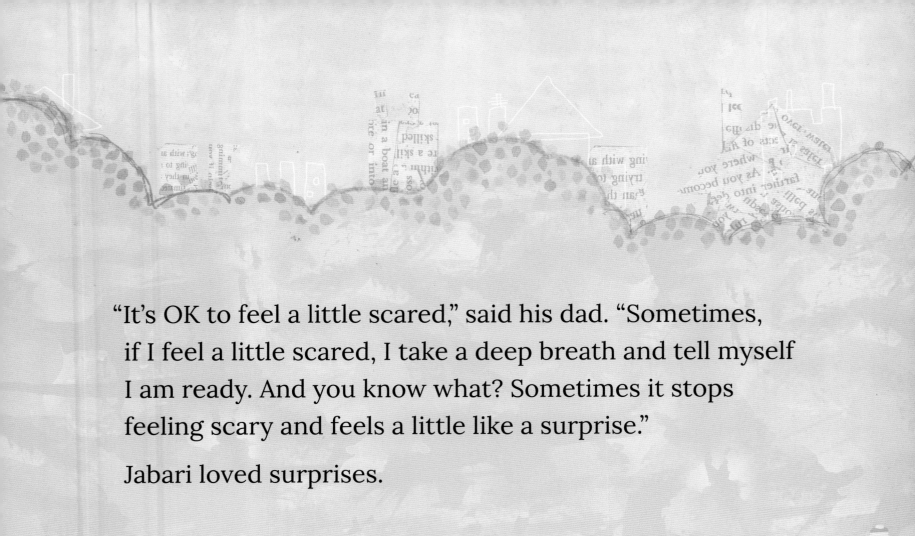

"It's OK to feel a little scared," said his dad. "Sometimes, if I feel a little scared, I take a deep breath and tell myself I am ready. And you know what? Sometimes it stops feeling scary and feels a little like a surprise."

Jabari loved surprises.

Jabari took a deep breath and felt it fill his body from the ends of his hair right down to the tips of his toes.

Jabari looked up.
He began to climb.

Up and up.
And up and up.

Until he got to the top.
Jabari stood up straight.

He walked all the way
to the end of the board.

His toes curled around the rough edge.

Jabari looked out, as far as he could see.
He felt like he was ready.

"I love surprises," he whispered.

He took a deep breath and spread his arms and bent his knees.

Then he sprang up!

Up off the board!

Flying!

Jabari hit the water with a

SP

Down,

down,

down he went.

And then back up!

"Jabari! You did it!" said his dad.

"I did it!" said Jabari. "I'm a great jumper!
 And you know what?"

"What?" said his dad.

"Surprise double backflip is next!"